THE GUILTLESS DESIRES

Sensual & Passionate Poems

By Rabiya Nizam 'Albina'

Published by

Power In Me Foundation

Book Name: The Guiltless Desires

Author: Rabiya Nizam 'Albina'

Format: Paperback

ISBN: 978-93-94749-41-2

Copyright:

Publisher

Power In Me Foundation, H.No. 531, MIG-21, Near Subhadra Memorial Hospital, Opp. SBI Colony, Ganiyari Road, Waidhan, District- Singrauli, Madhya Pradesh-486886. Email id: mpowerinme@gmail.com, Mobile: 8851537816.

Preface

Have you ever felt the beauty in the desire you have? The powerful energy it holds to put you together. Sensuality is one emotion that is not to be feared but to befriend it. As it drives you towards healing and creativity beyond you can think.

This book is a collection of 25 sensual and passionate poems that ooze the wonders of desires and take you to the wonderland of love and passion. Also, it means you do not need to feel guilty of your desires but to enjoy the ecstasy while it lasts in a pleasurable way.

Table Of Content

1. The Wine of lust

My heart becomes the Vessel of Amour
Brewin' the lusty wine of desire
And me, the Vinter of this ardor
played with the roaring fire,

I dreamt of playing with your curves,
Running my fingers through your tresses
And witness you disembogue like aromatic chocolate,
When against the wall our body presses.

I desiderate to explore thy realm,
Uninvaded and veiled from all eyes,
And merge like fire and Sun.
Making Eros Enthral.

And tasting your lips
like smothered cream,
I want my athirst territory to soak
In your endless stream.

2. Charm of the Dark

On this thunderous night
I crave to taste your honey lips,
And forget me in your arms
Lost in those eyes.

I wish to trace your body,
Like an artisan admire his art,
Savoring your lips every moment
Don't impede my love, let's start.

Let me smell that sweet fragrance
Spreading from your dewy flowers,
And let me fall like rain
In that parched terrain.

I wish to play with your silks
And Invade your reticent territory,
And hear you moaning in my ears,
"Don't break this bond free".

Entwining our fingers
I wanna push you to the wall,
And pinning your hand above
Savor those Bristol stars.

I wish you ink your love
With nails over my soma,
And your teeth leave those crimson
Trenchant spiel of night.

My lady! Whisper in my ear
That sweet melody of pain.
When that Vermilion leaves,
A bright alluring stain.

I covet to spend my night,
Melting in your arms.
And fàilte every dawn,
In your Canoodle O my love.

3. Kisses

Entangling our tongues
I savored your lips, your lips.
Melting like gold
Our heart skipped their beats.

Sweat beads on our course,
Coruscated like pearls
The fingers got tangled,
In those web of silky curls.

Your nudging blazed my inner world
Blazing like hell,
My hand traversed below,
To ring your glistening bell.
The aisle between the Crus,
Carved for the rain,
And the night reaches its denouement
When pleasure engulfed the terrain.

4. You owe my heart

You owe my heart

And the passion

Inflorescences in my mind.

You owe my heart

Coz I covet the raindrops

You flood in my parched caves.

You owe my heart

Coz the petrichor of your soused kiss

Permeate my soul.

You owe my heart

Coz the perfervid coitus

Melts the verglas of my flowers.

5. The Fire

Burn like Cinder
Blaze under desire,
Illuminating the neath
Rekindle this fire.

Let out aura surge
Annihilating all that's around
Let us melt like Wexan
Transfiguring ourselves to hound.

Come, my love
Let us unite
For I yearn to feel the spark
Of the Virite Vibes.

6. A Poem to remember

When poems are penned on skin
My lips and nails.
It scribbles down all the longings,
Engraving the anticipation
Of those long lonely nights,
Quenching all thirst of desire,
Plunging my soul in the realm of the divine,
Melting in your arms
I let go of my resentment
Encapsulating in your Universe,
You became my Eden!!

7. You never came back

Longing Transfigured into pain
Swaying trees reminded me of your torse
Desirous within my burned-like embers
As fragrance emitted from the gross.

Yearning for your touch.
A scintilla of seclusion emerged all night,
Till the dawn breaks in
Soaking the Orb in light.

Min bosom missed your touch of Eros
Parched land looked for the petrichor of sacred rain,
And here at my door, the night knocked
Unearthing my stabbing solitude again.

8. Tenderness

The slow surfing of your lips
On my body
Your palms flicking my domes
Tracing me like a sculpted Art,
Transfiguring my breezy urges into a typhoon.

Urging my Corse to sway with fire
That tides roar of raging desires.
Let me drink the nectar from your lips,
And let us take in darkness, a dip.

9. No More..

Soaring in your love
I felt that marvelling pain.
Forgetting all my uncertainties
And the engulfing anticipation
I got enticed by your scent
Your tongue ticking my petals
Transfiguring me into Xocotzins
To wander in the realm of lust.

10. 3434 Erotica

Igniting my passion
You wrapped around me
Those Velvety arms
Who do you blame now?

Our tongue twirled
And we tasted divine
Losing our minds
Who do you blame now?

You arouse fire,
And the desire burned
We clasped together
Who do you blame now?

The moans rang
In the beloved's ear,
We lived the night
Who do you blame now?

11. The raw love making

Eat me tonight,

Like melting chocolate.

Drink my honey,

Like Divine Elixir.

Merge with me,

So no void remains.

Paint the Silks,

With Vermilion stains.

12. And I sailed through the night

I sailed the night sea with the tide of our memories,
The flickering candlelight resembles our burning love
Through the Azure Sky, We fly together like passionate Dove.

I sailed the night sea with the tide of our memories,
When I slumber in the darkness, yet roused in your heart,
Veiled for the world, but for you I am stark.

I sailed the night sea with the tide of our memories,
When Hera played the melancholic notes on the Windy Zither,
In solitude drinking that concoction of separation,
I let the pain unwind.

I sailed the night sea with the tide of our memories,
When unrolling that sacred manuscript,
Inked with your affection, I deciphered the connections.

I sailed the night sea with the tide of our memories,

Biding my time, when the spring will bloom again,

And you will step back into my world!!

13. Satyriasis

Inexhaustible Volcanoes of passion,

Unwithering Eden of desires,

Dark terrain longing for an increased shower,

The shore of the body,

Dreaming to get adorned with silver pearls,

Domes coveting for those Emami's fingers,

Eyes to witness those flaring smiles

No, one season of rain can't please me,

I am crying out for Himeros for eternity.

14. O fleecy carrier

O fleecy carrier of heavenly pearls,
Can you bring me the words of desire from my beloved?
The song of cranial longing
Sung by my fair maiden?
Whose azure eyes smitten me
And now I am nestling her somewhere deep
Where she will never be lost.

O fleecy carrier of heavenly pearls,
Can you bring to her,
The essence of both lust and devotion, I have for her?
And shower that all,
Bringing my words to life,
Emanating the desire, tickling her core,
Can you drench her with all my yearning and Proclivity,
My heart brews in exile.

O fleecy carrier of heavenly pearls,
Can you make these winds hymn?

The songs of that silent night
When we crossed all worldly barriers
And I felt that life
In my once-cremated soul.

Because again I am moribund
With my eyes parched with pain
And heart with aggrieved thirst,
For I am forgetting my Aphrodite,
And the tune of her Zither,
Which once played the notes of buried passion.

O fleecy carrier of heavenly pearls,
Be my messenger of exile,
And bring back her words,
The words of life to me!!

15. When we meet

In the darkness, we met
With burning cinders of desires,
Heart throbbing,
And blood flowing like Magma, Unceased.
Those eyes which nestled our souls,
Leaving us both edgy and enlivened,
Your fingers traced my silhouette
Made me submerged more in your warmth,
And with those pleasurable throbbing
With those glistening red pearls on your chest and back,
Our love got solemnised.

16. Winters and You

As the nightfall
A gust of Winter Wind knocks at my Windowpane.
Rekindling the fire,
Which is dying without you,
bit by bit.

Concealed in my core
The Soma desiring for your warmth
The night flower waiting to get chafed
I spent the night in restiveness,
Impuissant to fondle you firmness,
I desire this gloom,
For never to come again,
As my garden whither
Without those sacred dews.

17. Him

With him, everything seems beautiful,

From rugged terrains

To the Copper Autumn leaves,

And those nights

When pain bled through my eyes

And I felt your lips on my lips

And your hands tighten the grip around me,

But, now they don't knock on my window anymore,

The haunting memories have turned into ashes,

Now all I listen to is the rustling silk

And the melting skin against each other.

The gashes, sores, and bites are all like a holy grail,

Because unconsciously we both have undressed,

Not just the body, but the soul and the heart,

And now as the naked body merges,

Everything intangibles edge becomes one

And solemnity of pain and pleasure

Builds a new tale.

18. Ah Man!

The taste of your lips

Your necks and the honey spot

Ah, Man! You killed me right there.

Grabbing your silk tresses and weaving through the curly tresses

And While Tasting you

The Moans I hear,

Ah, Man! You killed me right there.

Your orchid-red face, and the soft derriere

And the smile flicking like the candle's fire

Ah, Man! You killed me right there.

When that majestic glistening tarde slides in

The lust's river uproar,

Ah, Man! You killed me right there.

When you whisper in my ear

And tighten the grip on me,

And the pain merges with pleasure undefined,

Ah, Man! You killed me right there.

Your perfume envelops my senses

And we burned like Cinder, intense and bright,
The pearls drop off your face,
And upon reaching the depth,
You made my trust disappear,
Ah, Man! You killed me right there!!

19. The Rose Garden

Tresses entangled weaving the web
Fingers playing with mounts of flesh;
No wonder the garden was lush and rich,
With roses which were pink and red.

The Wanderer began to explore the terrain,
Having the valley aging without the rain,
He carefully caressed the land with touch,
And the roses bloomed with hush and blush.

The empyreal sang the song from Amor,
And Passion dancing on the fire floor,
The Eyes burned with unsung desires
When the carnal angels closed the doors.

20. The Dancing Fire

Those pair of eyes
And the throbbing yearnings in her,
Aren't the one of the Venus
But of the Aphrodite

His passion searing like the Thar
And his lips,
restless to savor the love
In that darkness of the night
His concupiscence embodied Eros.

And then begin their sermon
For which they were longing,
The fingers traced the petal
And the domes
And the shafts.
Entwining like the nestle of a dove

The rim of those wine glasses touched each other
And emptied those wine

Relishing the taste of each other,

They no longer knew who remains

The Soma no longer remains ungashed

And the crimson verdict of love oozed out

And then it busted

What was once the Scotch mist and the cinder

None, intending to stop but to engulf the other,

And then the Fire Danced in the Thunder.

Until there were no void remains.

21. Melting Candles

We melted down
Like the Candles
And bursted in heat, so bright
Scattering all the fire
From the eyes and the flirting lips.
Your whispers thundered
Like the bolts in the storms
Meant on burning all
The soft and silken bod.
Entwining our tongues
We tasted each other's breathe
The locked emotions poured
In silence they quethe.
The Veins down there,
Turned hot like molten iron
Scalding my flowers
And making me yearn.
Your pearls marked my territory
And my claws marked your bod.
The purple lavender bloomed

On my chest and your throat.

We solemnized our Union under sky

Merging, we turn to one

Then you laid on the floral bed

While I enjoyed the fervent ride.

22. Spice it up

As I inhaled your breath.

You smelled like a cinnamon, Wet and sweet.

And I tasted your lips, the flavoury saffron.

Let's entwine our somas, Like the dewy honeycomb.

And burn in passion like the bay leaves.

I tasted the nutmeg on your soft bosom.

Tasting the mace on your navel, while playing with my tongue.

Your skin shines bright, like the sprinks on green chillies.

And your moans enraptured me, like the turmeric, so deep.

Our skin rubbed together, like sandalwood with mortar.

That left some deep, some shallow peppery scars.

When I reached the mystical destination,

Going in through the magic door

I felt the sweet and sour like plum, tingling and exciting me more.

We spattered like fennel, fenugreek, and chives.

Our love was not usual,

But the dance of spices.

23. Sandalwood Palace

I scratched the timbers

With those ebony nail

My heart throbbed

And the Veins pulsed

The beads of the sea dripping

Soaked not just the body but the soul.

And I traced down

The art of the god

In the midst of the night

When our hearts roared nothing

But the name of Eros,

And I smelled your flowers

The Sandalwood palace,

As it was in Kamasutra

I felt the fragrance

The taste

And your bosom was like the shore

Amidst of the roaring sea of desire

You burst with passion

And then our union was inevitable

Like The Night song of lust for the Psyche!!

24. Exotic Taste

You spilled over me
Like the late autumn
And I embraced you
Like the willows of the woods
Bracing each other
We were coveted by the world

I wished you to come down to me
Like the lioness
And I wanted to worship
Your ethereal beauty

I smell you
And I taste your dripping honey
You marked me yours
You marked me yours
As I took your body tours.

The valley and ravines
And their exotic taste

The passion and sweet tooth

Over your navel route

25. Erotic Charm

Don't whisper my name
Don't hiss in my ears
Because I won't hold back
And that's what I fear

I will make you melt
And moan and screech
I will taste your melon
And feel your peach.

I enhanced the fragrance
From your tiny lips
I want to go wild
And feel the kinky bits.

I wanted your taste in my mouth
Yearning like a fleeting cloud
Loneliness pained me,
No wonder I wandered
In search of you

From North to South.

And no I have you in my arms
Enchanted with your erotic charm
I can taste your flowers
And slide in you
No wonder I am here
Now, drinking heavenly dew.

Supporting Cause

The author of the book supports the mental health issues and believes it is high time that the world starts talking about it. There is a grave need to understand this invisible aspect of one's life and build support mechanism to make it easy for those suffering to easily share their pain.

She is even volunteer to supporting the cause of advocating about need to create positive community mindset regarding mental health by Power In Me Foundation. As the NGO, constantly talks about need for mental health support even for the patients with rare diseases and their care givers. It is important to share a support to these vulnerable parts of the society and ensure a good quality of life for even them.

About Author

Rabiya Nizam 'Albina' is a profound writer with good experience as a content writer and a teacher helping unwind the young minds. She loves to speak from the heart which also shows into her writing. She talks and writes on topics of social issues and often women oriented content is seen into her expressions.

About Publisher

Power In Me Foundation is the publisher for this book titled 'Guiltless Desires' by Rabiya Nizam with Albina as her pen name. The Trust works on sustainable development model. It is established to work for the welfare of the people with rare diseases and their families. Publishing is one of the activities to help raise funds to carry out the activities aimed to creating awareness about various rare diseases, provide scholarships for studies, to provide for livelihood training, to provide for healthcare training, to establish centres for their care and various other objectives for social causes.

The authors associated with us follow the same vision to make the society a better place through their creative writing. We encourage raw talents with time-to-time guidance and exposure through our creative platform Ruh-E-Mohabbat by supporting and promoting them.

For any query on our publishing services, or supporting our cause to create awareness about rare diseases while empowering them you can reach us at mpowerinme@ gmail.com. You can even call/whatsapp at +91-8851537816.

www.ingramcontent.com/pod-product-compliance
Lightning Source LLC
LaVergne TN
LVHW010123170826
845678LV00012B/2570

* 9 7 8 9 3 9 4 7 4 9 4 1 2 *